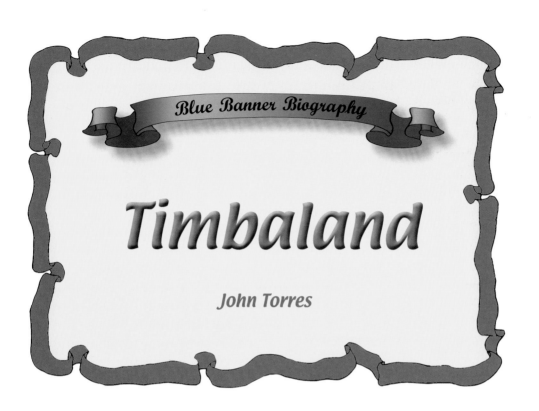

Blue Banner Biography

Timbaland

John Torres

Mitchell Lane
PUBLISHERS

P.O. Box 196
Hockessin, Delaware 19707
Visit us on the web: www.mitchelllane.com
Comments? email us: mitchelllane@mitchelllane.com

Mitchell Lane PUBLISHERS

Printing   1   2   3   4   5   6   7   8   9

Blue Banner Biographies

Akon	Alan Jackson	Alicia Keys
Allen Iverson	Ashanti	Ashlee Simpson
Ashton Kutcher	Avril Lavigne	Bernie Mac
Beyoncé	Bow Wow	Brett Favre
Britney Spears	Carrie Underwood	Chris Brown
Chris Daughtry	Christina Aguilera	Christopher Paul Curtis
Ciara	Clay Aiken	Condoleezza Rice
Corbin Bleu	Daniel Radcliffe	David Ortiz
Derek Jeter	Eminem	Eve
Fergie (Stacy Ferguson)	50 Cent	Gwen Stefani
Ice Cube	Jamie Foxx	Ja Rule
Jay-Z	Jennifer Lopez	Jessica Simpson
J. K. Rowling	Johnny Depp	JoJo
Justin Berfield	Justin Timberlake	Kanye West
Kate Hudson	Keith Urban	Kelly Clarkson
Kenny Chesney	Lance Armstrong	Lindsay Lohan
Mariah Carey	Mario	Mary J. Blige
Mary-Kate and Ashley Olsen	Michael Jackson	Miguel Tejada
Missy Elliott	Nancy Pelosi	Nelly
Orlando Bloom	P. Diddy	Paris Hilton
Peyton Manning	Queen Latifah	Rihanna
Ron Howard	Rudy Giuliani	Sally Field
Sean Kingston	Selena	Shakira
Shirley Temple	Soulja Boy Tell 'Em	Taylor Swift
Timbaland	Tim McGraw	Toby Keith
Usher	Vanessa Anne Hudgens	Zac Efron

Library of Congress Cataloging-in-Publication Data
Torres, John Albert.
  Timbaland / by John A. Torres.
    p. cm. — (Blue banner biographies)
  Includes bibliographical references, discography, and index.
  ISBN 978-1-58415-671-0 (library bound)
  1. Timbaland (Musician) 2. Rap musicians—United States—Biography—Juvenile literature.
I. Title.
  ML3930.T577T67 2009
  782.421649092—dc22
  [B]
                                                                                    2008008064

ABOUT THE AUTHOR: John A. Torres is an award-winning journalist covering social issues for *Florida Today*. John has also written more than 40 books for various publishers, including *Marc Anthony, Mia Hamm,* and *Meet Our New Student from Haiti* for Mitchell Lane Publishers. In his spare time, John likes playing sports, going to theme parks, and fishing with his children, stepchildren, and wife, Jennifer.

PUBLISHER'S NOTE: The following story has been thoroughly researched, and to the best of our knowledge represents a true story. While every possible effort has been made to ensure accuracy, the publisher will not assume liability for damages caused by inaccuracies in the data and makes no warranty on the accuracy of the information contained herein. This story has not been authorized or endorsed by Timbaland.

Rapper, songwriter, and producer Timbaland was nominated for five Grammy Awards in 2007. By then he was also running his own record company, Mosley Music Group (MMG). He says: "You can accomplish anything you put your mind to if you stay persistent and disciplined."

A Household Name

Recording artists and entertainers dream of having the kind of year, the kind of success, and the kind of impact that Timothy Mosley had in 2007.

Huh? Never heard of Timothy Mosley? Chances are unless you've been living under a rock, you have heard some of the most played, most popular rhythms, melodies, riffs, and grooves that he has created. If you've heard a song by Nelly Furtado, danced to one by Missy Elliott, or grooved your way through a Justin Timberlake chart-topper, then you have definitely been exposed to the world of Timothy Mosley.

In 2007 he not only had three consecutive number 1 singles in the U.S., but he also became just the fourth artist to hold both the number 1 and number 2 spots on the Australian music chart at the same time. The last person to do that was Madonna in 1985.

Oh yeah, he also appeared on the hit television soap opera *One Life to Live.*

You probably know him by his professional name, Timbaland. And despite his little foray into daytime television, Timbaland remains committed to music. Even the soap opera, he says, was about his art. "This is a new experience for me," he said about being on television. "I am looking forward to having a great time and sharing my music."

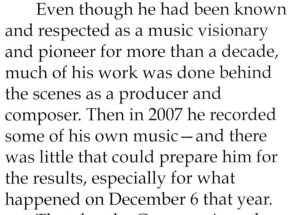

Timbaland admitted to being just a little bitter that he was not nominated for Producer of the Year in 2002.

Even though he had been known and respected as a music visionary and pioneer for more than a decade, much of his work was done behind the scenes as a producer and composer. Then in 2007 he recorded some of his own music — and there was little that could prepare him for the results, especially for what happened on December 6 that year.

That day the Grammy Award nominations were announced, and Timothy "Timbaland" Mosley was honored with five. Sure, he had been nominated before, but this was different. This time Timbaland was being recognized for efforts out in front of his music, not just for work in the studio.

He was nominated for Record of the Year for Justin Timberlake's "What Goes Around . . . Comes Around"; Best Pop Collaboration for "Give It to Me," featuring both Timberlake and Nelly Furtado; Best Dance Recording for Justin Timberlake's "Love Stoned/I Think She Knows"; Best Rap Song for "Ayo Technology" by 50 Cent; and Nonclassical Producer of the Year.

The Grammy Award is the most prestigious prize in the music business and coveted by just about anyone who makes music for a living. In the past, however — in typical

Timbaland fashion—Mosley shrugged off award nominations as nothing more than a popularity contest.

"The people that get the most press . . . those are the ones that win," he said in 2002. "It isn't real music like it used to be. [When] Carlos Santana won—that was a real Grammy." Timbaland was referring to the Grammy awarded to longtime rocker Santana for his 1999 album *Supernatural.*

Timbaland admitted to being just a little bitter that he was not nominated for a Grammy for Producer of the Year in 2002, even though he had produced several popular and award-winning songs. "I don't play the politic game enough to be in it," he said, adding that he preferred to spend his energy simply on making music.

Although he did not win any Grammys in 2002, Timbaland did take home two Billboard R&B Hip Hop Awards that year: for Songwriter of the Year and Producer of the Year.

Some of what Timbaland was feeling could be traced to the simple fact that he wanted some recognition for what he was doing. Even by 2007, he was known more for his production and songwriting skills than for being an artist in his own right. No one talks about the producer of their favorite record. They usually talk about the singer or the band. For producers, that can be frustrating.

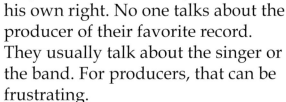

Timbaland insists that the only thing he cares about is making music that people like and that will last.

Still, Timbaland insists that the only thing he cares about is making music that people like and that will last. While he has helped artists in the rock, hip-hop, pop, and rhythm and blues fields make their mark on the charts, there is something Timbaland admits to wanting to accomplish before he's through: writing a classic.

"[I'd like to make a record] with the Rolling Stones because they make classic records," he said. "And I need one of those classic 'Titanic' records."

Of course, classics don't become classics overnight—and Timbaland may have already produced one. Many music fans and critics alike already consider *Justified*—a Timbaland collaboration with Justin Timberlake—to be a classic recording. And someone who is as talented as Timothy Mosley—er, Timbaland—is bound to come up with a few more classics by the time he is finished making music.

Tim the Deejay

On March 10, 1971, thirty-seven years before Timbaland provided pulsating rhythms and a pounding downbeat for a song called "Bounce," featuring Missy Elliott, Justin Timberlake, and rapper Dr. Dre, Timothy Z. Mosley was born in Norfolk, Virginia.

Mosley had a typical childhood, growing up on the sometimes rough streets of Norfolk. He says it doesn't matter at all where he grew up because there was someone, along with his mother, who provided a great foundation for who he would later become. "I don't know how living in Virginia shaped me," he said. "God shaped me." Because of God's help, he believes, he could have been raised anywhere and still found his passion for music.

Besides giving him a Christian upbringing, Mosley's mother, Latrice Mosley, bought him a gift when he turned fourteen that would shape him more than anything else on earth. In 1985, she bought him a Casio keyboard.

Though he always had an interest in music, now he was hooked. He would sit in his room and teach himself how to play. One riff after another would roll off his fingers as he looked for something new, something slick and hip. Then he started to learn drums and guitar as well, exploring different sounds.

God, his mother, and someone he met while a student at Salem High School of Virginia Beach would guide the musical giant who would come out of Norfolk, Virginia. One of Timbaland's best friends during high school was R&B singer Missy Elliott of nearby Portsmouth. They would talk about music together and their dreams. Soon, music became *the* dream.

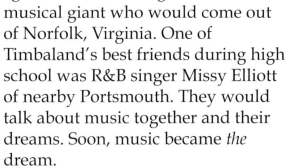

While in high school, Timbaland started working as a deejay and called himself Timmy Tim.

While in high school, Timbaland started working as a deejay and called himself Timmy Tim or DJ Tiny Tim. When he wasn't spinning records and learning from the sounds that were making the airwaves rock, Mosley was making music with Elliott. In fact, they recorded an unreleased album together while they were still high school students.

Their music did not make them instant superstars, so Elliott formed a group with some friends called Sista. Timmy Tim formed a group with friends Melvin Barcliff and Pharrell Williams called Surrounded by Idiots, or SBI.

By the early 1990s, Elliott had an inside connection: She was able to get an audition with Devante Swing, who was a member of the hit R&B group Jodeci. Elliott brought her talented musical friend Mosley with her. Swing was taken with both musical talents. He noticed Mosley was wearing the popular Timberland construction boots and promptly nicknamed him Timbaland. The name stuck.

Swing decided to sign the two rising stars to his label, which was affiliated with Elektra Records. Swing's musical family included big names like Ginuwine, whose career would really take off once he got into a recording studio with the confident kid named after a brand of boots.

Together Timbaland and Elliott started writing songs together. People in the music business were soon praising the duo for their prolific songwriting and unique styles. They would usher in a new form of hip-hop sound that borrowed heavily from rock, alternative, electronica, and other synthesizer-grounded sounds.

After success with Ginuwine's "Pony," Timbaland teamed up with Elliott to write and produce four songs on

Record producer Timbaland is clearly at home in this New York music studio in 1998. More than 10 years later, he was still one of the hottest producers in hip-hop.

Timbaland and popular hip-hop artist Missy Elliott would produce award-winning music together. They started writing songs and working together when they were high school friends.

rising superstar Aaliyah's *One in a Million.* The recordings were different than anything else. They included sounds like insects and crying babies that made them even more unique. The album was a smashing success. It went double platinum, meaning it sold more than two million copies.

With that success in hand, Elliott was given the go-ahead to record her first solo album. Of course, there was only one person in the world she would allow to produce her debut: her best friend, Timbaland.

Supa Dupa Fly

Missy Elliott and the record company executives could not have come up with a better match to produce her first album, *Supa Dupa Fly*. The album catapulted Elliott to superstardom and made it to number 3 on the Billboard charts. The album "showcased Elliott's often funny lyrical content, her feminist stance and her singing ability," commented music writer Malcolm Venable of the *Virginian-Pilot* newspaper.

Soon other artists began asking Timbaland to help them come up with a new sound or something exciting for them to record. The soft-spoken Timbaland offered no answer when asked a few years later about the creative process that allows him to come up with original sounds, rhythms, and grooves. "The sounds just come from whatever I'm thinking," he said. "It's all in my head, not influenced by anybody. I'm just blessed that my ear is good."

Shortly after the Missy Elliott success, Timbaland recorded his first album as an artist in his own right. He contacted his old friend and bandmate Melvin Barcliff, who was already rapping under the name Magoo. Magoo said some of their sound was New York influenced with a lot of East Coast rapping styles in it. The album *Welcome to Our World* was a moderate hit. While it didn't put the names Timbaland and Magoo on the top of the charts, the album showed people that Timbaland's talents went beyond mixing the sounds, inserting beats or rhythms, and trying to create a catchy melody. He could rap as well.

After trying his hand at being a recording artist, Timbaland returned to his bread and butter: producing songs for other people.

Though the album was filled with what has become the typical Timbaland sound — heavy beats and syncopated rhythms — it wasn't a typical rap album. It showed Timbaland's willingness to experiment with other styles of music. Perhaps that's why so many artists from different styles of music have wanted to work with him.

While he was recording with Magoo, Timbaland remarked that he did not want to be tied down to the title of producer, songwriter, or artist. He called himself an entertainer. And this entertainer seemed to have an endless supply of ideas for songs.

"I've made lots of sounds," he said. "I have different flavors that I can pick and choose from with an artist. It's like a candy shop. Most producers don't or can't do that and that's why they stick to hip-hop. I just don't do one genre. I bring in that hardcore beat and put it with other music. It could be country or rock. I just love music. I do music for the fans. I want to lift the fans up."

After trying his hand at being a recording artist, Timbaland returned to his bread and butter: producing songs

Timbaland has produced hit songs for Missy Elliott (right), Nas (center), and Aaliyah (left), including "You Won't See Me Tonight" by Nas featuring Aaliyah in 1999.

for other people. He produced megahits for many artists, but it was his 1998 collaboration with Jay-Z that won the most acclaim. Timbaland's direction turned the songs "Jigga What, Jigga Who," and "Big Pimpin' " into huge chart-busting hits. Jay-Z's album was a multiplatinum success.

In 2001, Timbaland and Missy Elliott would come together again and produce an album for their old friend Aaliyah. A critical and commercial success, the album *Aaliyah* was a top-10 smash around the world.

Unfortunately, it would be Aaliyah's last album. She died in a plane crash a few weeks after its release. Her death would convince Timbaland to change his lifestyle.

Soon after producing Aaliyah's album, Timbaland started growing fidgety and impatient from what he perceived as a

At the 2001 MTV Video Music Awards held at the Metropolitan Opera House in New York, Missy Elliott, Ginuwine, and Timbaland try to hold back tears as they remember their friend Aaliyah, who was killed in a plane crash on August 25 that year.

lack of recognition. He wanted some of the credit for making these artists as popular as they were becoming. Not many people read the notes on the case of a compact disc to see who did what. They had no idea who Timbaland was.

He also felt that he was inventing styles and sounds that others were copying without giving him the credit he deserved. "I changed radio for the nineties," he said. "A star can bite [steal] my sound and blow up off my sound, but I feel like I still don't get the props [awards] I deserve."

Life Changes

While he may seem gruff and tough on the outside, Timbaland is actually shy and quiet—he's a man of few words. And even though he moved his base of operations to the high life of Miami once he hit it big, friends and music watchers say that he still prefers a low-key lifestyle over one of glamour and excitement.

While the early 2000s were successful for Timbaland, there were other things going through his mind that he tried to balance while still producing music for others. He helped produce another album for Elliott, whom he refers to as his sister. They also wrote a tremendously popular song called "Get Ur Freak On," which raced up the music charts all over the world and became a catchphrase in clubs and on radio and television stations.

He also found time to go back into the recording studio as an artist and record a second album with Magoo. The album, *Indecent Proposal*, used a lot of different rhythms, drums, and samples. Samples are snippets of other songs that are used in a repetitive or very sparse way to sound like something new.

For this second album between the friends, Magoo knew to let Timbaland handle the production. After all, he was the expert. "[We have] an equal say. Tim obviously does the production," said Magoo. "But there are no egos in the studio with us. I let him be the coach. We never have arguments."

Magoo added that there has never been any jealousy between the old high school bandmates, even though Timbaland has become much more successful than Magoo. "I'm happy for him," he said. "When we started, we just wanted to say we had a record out, and now look at us."

Much like their first album, the second was received well but did not make the two friends recording superstars. Maybe it was destined that Timbaland's greatest success would be crafting the sounds of others, and not in recording his own performances.

> *Maybe it was destined that Timbaland's greatest success would be crafting the sounds of others, and not in recording his own performances.*

In 2002, Timbaland decided to collaborate with someone who was branching out on his own after being part of one of the most popular boy bands ever. Justin Timberlake, who had been one of the lead singers of 'N Sync, was ready to try a solo recording career.

Many former teen stars in popular musical acts have had a hard time establishing a successful career on their own. But for Timberlake, the timing was right. He had ended a romantic relationship with pop queen Britney Spears and had started seeing Hollywood actress Cameron Diaz. Whatever that meant for his private life, in public, it kept his name in the newspapers and gossip magazines. Meanwhile, the hottest producer in the business — Timbaland — was free to work on a project with him.

The result was *Justified* — one of the hottest albums ever, and one that catapulted Timberlake into instant superstardom. Timbaland's work on the album — especially the slow thumpy beat and lyrical hooks on "Cry Me a River" — was amazing. The song and album became instant classics.

By this time, Timbaland started feeling rundown. He was worried about his health. He was more than 100 pounds overweight and did not want his health to suffer. The death of his friend Aaliyah profoundly affected his view of life. He realized he wanted to keep living for a long time.

Timbaland and pop superstar Justin Timberlake perform "My Love/ SexyBack" at the 2006 MTV Video Music Awards. Timbaland has helped write and produce several smash hits for Timberlake — who has returned the favor by lending his talent to many of Timbaland's projects.

He was also feeling burned out. The hectic pace of the music industry was starting to get to him. He was growing weary of the constant interaction with so many people all the time. He retreated to his Miami home (he also had one in Virginia) to heal his mind and to lose some weight.

With faith and talent, Timbaland knew he would get a chance to rise to the top again. It wouldn't take him long.

"It's more that I got tired of people," he said. "I wanted to train and lose all the weight I had gained. And I knew I wanted to do something different musically."

The life change worked. He trimmed down and started working out. Timbaland even considered entering some bodybuilding competitions. His mind was clearer as well.

In the music business, taking a break can have a disastrous effect. Popularity is fleeting, and you are only as good or as popular as your last hit record. Timbaland was out of sight, and soon he was out of mind. Record companies that had been so eager to get him into their recording studios were wondering if he had lost his edge.

Having people lose confidence in him became very tough for Timbaland. To get through it, he reached back down to the strength in his foundation and his upbringing: God.

"It's prayer," he said. "I had a lot of people praying for me. They saw me in my crisis stage when stuff was just going downhill for me. I'd do something, it wouldn't work and I couldn't understand why. But I kept my faith and belief in God."

Timbaland dances with his sister Cheryl at his 2005 Super Birthday Bash. His younger brother, Garland, also known as Sebastian, is also in the hip-hop business. Besides being a rapper himself, he has worked at MMG and written several songs with Timbaland. Little is known about Timbaland's relationship with other family members.

With faith and talent, Timbaland knew he would get a chance to rise to the top again. It wouldn't take him long.

On Top

*I*t's not as if Timbaland had stopped producing hits while he was taking his "break." It's just that he had slowed down a bit. He responded to the critics by deciding to come back strong, and he wasn't afraid of speaking his mind.

"You have a job like I have a job and you shouldn't put me down because I'm not doing what you think I should," he said. "It hurts when people put you down. But I came back with a vengeance."

Someone else whose star had lost a bit of luster was Justin Timberlake. He had recorded a few things but was unable to recapture the magic of *Justified.* Then there was an unfortunate incident—a "wardrobe malfunction"—with Janet Jackson during the half-time concert at the 2004 Super Bowl. Timberlake received a lot of criticism for the display.

When he teamed up with Timbaland to do a song— "Good Foot"—for the movie *Shark Tale,* both men were trying to revive their careers. Timbaland was concerned that Timberlake was not himself and that he had lost his confidence. He was even considering giving acting a try and putting his music on the back burner.

"He also didn't like the way he was sounding, so he started doing movies," Timbaland recalled. "I boosted him up, saying, 'Don't think that way; I'm here for you. Let's go back and do this.' "

He continued, "We both got our confidence back at the same time and that makes a lot of difference. We knocked the negativity out and surrounded ourselves with positive stuff. We just kept it moving."

The resulting album, *FutureSex/LoveSounds*, was a recording success for both Timberlake and Timbaland. Timbaland was featured on several songs, including "Chop Me Up" and "SexyBack," which became a number one hit song. The album went multiplatinum, and Timbaland won two Grammy Awards for his work on it. He was back and in demand once again.

Timbaland presents Timberlake with one of four awards at the 2007 MTV Video Music Awards Show. Timbaland has greatly influenced Timberlake's successful singing career.

His personal life was also starting to fly high. Timbaland started dating his publicist, Monique Idlett. The two fell in love, and in October 2007 he asked her to marry him. The proposal was made in front of family and friends when he presented Monique with a stunning diamond ring at her baby shower. In November, the happy couple was blessed with the birth of a baby girl, Reign.

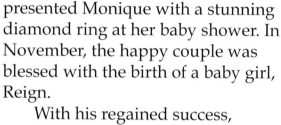

In 2007, Timbaland finally broke through as a recording artist. His solo album, Timbaland Presents: Shock Value, was a smash.

With his regained success, Timbaland could have chosen to work with anyone from a large group of people. But there was one singer/ songwriter—Nelly Furtado—whom he knew personally and who had always intrigued him. There was a quality to her voice that he actually called magical. "Nelly has a real sense of adventure, so many ideas and a special talent for hearing melodies," he said.

Like many of the artists with whom Timbaland has worked, Furtado had a smash debut record but then followed it up with a disappointing second album. She needed a hit, and she needed a new sound. In the studio, she and Timbaland just clicked.

"I do know that Timbaland and I have chemistry and our songs have a simplicity to them, an innocence, and humans relate," she said, adding that working with Timbaland provided her with an opportunity to reinvent herself. "Tim has the same voracious appetite for music that I do."

The album, *Loose*, became a multiplatinum international success. It was a hit record in at least twenty-four countries.

Not only has Timbaland helped stars become megastars, he has also helped other people in need. In 2003, he worked together with Timberlake and Elliott to write "The World Is Ours: AIDS Anthem," to help raise awareness for AIDS relief in Africa. "I see this as a passing of the torch," Timbaland said at the time. "I will use the legendary model of 'We Are the World,' but update it in a way that works for the trends of the industry today. Just as Quincy Jones, Lionel Richie and Michael Jackson did twenty years ago, we will create an anthem with today's most talented artists to

Timbaland speaks at a media conference for the YouthAIDS Benefit Gala. This group is working in more than 70 countries to educate and protect children from HIV – the virus that causes AIDS.

produce a song that will bring the world's attention to the AIDS pandemic."

Since then, he has done other work for YouthAIDS, including designing a T-shirt for their Fashion Against AIDS campaign. Part of the profits from the shirts would benefit the YouthAIDS organization.

In 2007, Timbaland finally broke through as a recording artist. His solo album, *Timbaland Presents: Shock Value,* was a smash both critically and commercially.

The album, which is autobiographical in nature, was something Timbaland had been thinking about for a while. It took a push from Timberlake to make the dream a reality.

"I had some of this album in mind before I hit with Justin and Nelly," Timbaland said. "But Justin solidified it for me. He said I needed to do something for myself."

One of the most appealing aspects of the album is all the guests whom Timbaland was able to feature, and who added their own special talents. In addition to Missy Elliott, Justin Timberlake, and Nelly Furtado, artists Elton John, Fall Out Boy, the Hives, and OneRepublic perform on the album.

OneRepublic's lead singer Ryan Tedder called working with Timbaland a very natural thing. "With Timbaland there are no rules," he said. "We can go in any direction we want to."

Maybe that's what helps make him so good, so successful.

> **With no boundaries and no stereotypes holding him down, maybe Timbaland has not yet reached his potential.**

Timbaland and Nelly Furtado accept a Teen Choice Award for their song "Promiscuous." Timbaland always liked the quality of Furtado's voice. In 2007 he produced several recordings for her as she returned to the top of the charts. The two have spoken about forming a rock group together.

Nelly Furtado once referred to him as a musical outlaw. With no boundaries and no stereotypes holding him down, maybe Timbaland has not yet reached his potential — although it's hard to imagine anyone gaining more respect and popularity than Timbaland has in the popular music industry.

"My music consumes me," he said, "but I'm just enjoying life."

He sure is.

1971   Timothy Z. Mosley, Timbaland, is born on March 10 in Norfolk, Virginia.

1985   His mother buys him a Casio keyboard.

1986   He attends Salem High School in Virginia Beach.

1988   Timbaland records an unreleased album with his friend Missy Elliott.

1996   Timbaland produces an album for Ginuwine and teams up with Elliott to produce songs for Aaliyah's album.

1997   Timbaland and Magoo make the top 40 with a song called "Up Jumps Da' Boogie."

1998   Timbaland produces a smash hit song on an album for Jay-Z.

2001   Timbaland and Missy Elliott record "Get Ur Freak On," a hit song that sparks an international catchphrase. He and Magoo release *Indecent Proposal* in November.

2002   Timbaland works with Justin Timberlake on the album *Justified*; he takes a break to lose 100 pounds and regain his mental health.

2003   Timbaland and Magoo release *Under Construction Part II*. Timbaland, Timberlake, and Missy Elliott work together to write "The World Is Ours: AIDS Anthem."

2006   Timbaland teams up with Timberlake again on *Future Sex/ Love Sounds*. He also produces Nelly Furtado's album *Loose*, catapulting her to stardom. He starts up a new record label called MMG, for Mosley Music Group.

2007   Timbaland proposes marriage to Monique Idlett; their daughter, Reign, is born in November. Timbaland wins two Grammy awards. His album *Timbaland Presents: Shock Value* goes platinum.

2008   Timbaland wins a Grammy for Best Dance Recording with Justin Timberlake for "LoveStoned/I Think She Knows," one of the five awards for which he was nominated. Timbaland's collaboration with OneRepublic on the song "Apologize" goes to the top of the Billboard Hot Adult Top 40. Timbaland and other musical artists design their own shirts to raise awareness for AIDS in a project called Fashion Against AIDS.

ACHIEVEMENTS

Albums
2008   *Timbaland Presents: Shock Value II*
2007   *Remix & Soundtrack Collection*
           Timbaland Presents: Shock Value
2003   *Under Construction, Part II* (Timbaland & Magoo)
2001   *Indecent Proposal* (Timbaland & Magoo)
1998   *Tim's Bio: Life from da Bassment*
1997   *Welcome to Our World* (Timbaland & Magoo)

Top-10 Singles
2007   "Apologize" (Remix) (feat. OneRepublic)
           "The Way I Are" (feat. Keri Hilson & D.O.E.)
           "Give It To Me" (feat. Justin Timberlake & Nelly Furtado)

Top-10 Singles as Featured Performer
2008   "4 Minutes" (Madonna, also feat. Justin Timberlake)
2007   "Ayo Technology" (50 Cent, also feat. Justin Timberlake)
2006   "SexyBack" (Justin Timberlake)
2004   "Promiscuous" (Nelly Furtado)
2001   "Ugly" (Bubba Sparxxx)
1998   "Are You That Somebody" (Aaliyah)

Artists and Groups Associated with Timbaland

50 Cent	Flo Rida	LL Cool J	Nephew
Aaliyah	The Game	Lloyd Banks	Omarion
Ashlee Simpson	Ginuwine	Ludacris	OneRepublic
Beck	Jay-Z	M.I.A.	Petey Pablo
Bone Thugs-N-Harmony	Jennifer Lopez	Madonna	Playa
	Jodeci	Magoo	Pussycat Dolls
Brandy	JoJo	Mary J. Blige	Rouge
Bubba Sparxxx	Justin Timberlake	Missy Elliott	Snoop Dogg
D.O.E.	Keri Hilson	Ms. Jade	Static Major
Danja	Kiley Dean	NLT	Tweet
Duran Duran	Lil' Kim	Nas	Usher
Elton John	Limp Bizkit	Nelly Furtado	Utada Hikaru

FURTHER READING

If you enjoyed this book about Timbaland, you might also enjoy these Blue Banner Biographies about some of the people with whom he has worked:

Bankston, John. *Jay-Z.* Hockessin, Delaware: Mitchell Lane Publishers, 2005.

Bankston, John. *Missy Elliott.* Hockessin, Delaware: Mitchell Lane Publishers, 2004.

Boone, Mary. *50 Cent.* Hockessin, Delaware: Mitchell Lane Publishers, 2007.

Kjelle, Marylou Morano. *Ashlee Simpson.* Hockessin, Delaware: Mitchell Lane Publishers, 2006.

Menard, Valerie. *Jennifer Lopez.* Hockessin, Delaware: Mitchell Lane Publishers, 2004.

Orr, Tamra. *JoJo.* Hockessin, Delaware: Mitchell Lane Publishers, 2008.

Torres, Jennifer. *Mary J. Blige.* Hockessin, Delaware: Mitchell Lane Publishers, 2008.

Torres, John. *Usher.* Hockessin, Delaware: Mitchell Lane Publishers, 2006.

Tracy, Kathleen. *Justin Timberlake.* Hockessin, Delaware: Mitchell Lane Publishers, 2008.

Works Consulted

Anderman, Joan. "The New Nelly," *The Boston Globe* and *The Virginia-Pilot,* May 31, 2007.

Dansby, Andrew. "JT, Timbaland Help 'World'; New Single to Benefit AIDS Charity," *Rolling Stone,* October 30, 2003; http://www.rollingstone.com/artists/justintimberlake/articles/story/5936847/jt_timbaland_help_world

Doty, Meriah. "Hiphop Trailblazer Timbaland Resists Grammy Hype," CNN.com. http://archives.cnn.com/2002/SHOWBIZ/Music/02/25/gram.timbaland/index.html?related

Mitchell, Gail. "The Beat Goes On: Timbaland," Billboard.com, March 3, 2007.

Rowland, Marijke. "OneRepublic Scores Hit before Album," *The [Marysville, California] Appeal-Democrat*, December 8, 2007.

Tayler, Letta. "Chairman of the (Sound) Board," *Newsday*, May 6, 2001.

"Timbaland to Make Soap Debut," *WENN Entertainment*, News Wire Service, September 20, 2007.

Venable, Malcolm. "He's a Hitmaking Producer Who Likes to Stay Low Key." *The Virginian-Pilot*, April 3, 2003.

———. "Timbaland & Magoo: Straight Outta VA," *The Virginian-Pilot*, November 20, 2003.

On the Internet

Mosley Music Group
http://www.mosleymusicgroup.net/

MTV Artist: Timbaland
http://www.mtv.com/music/artist/timbaland/artist.jhtml

Timbaland: Official Site
http://www.timbalandmusic.com/

VH1 Artists: Timbaland
http://www.vh1.com/artists/az/timbaland/bio.jhtml

Youth AIDS
http://www.youthaids.org

INDEX